This book belongs to:

_____

Disney

Frozen

The Story of Anna & Elsa

Disney

Frozen

❄

The Story of Anna & Elsa

Disney PRESS

Los Angeles • New York

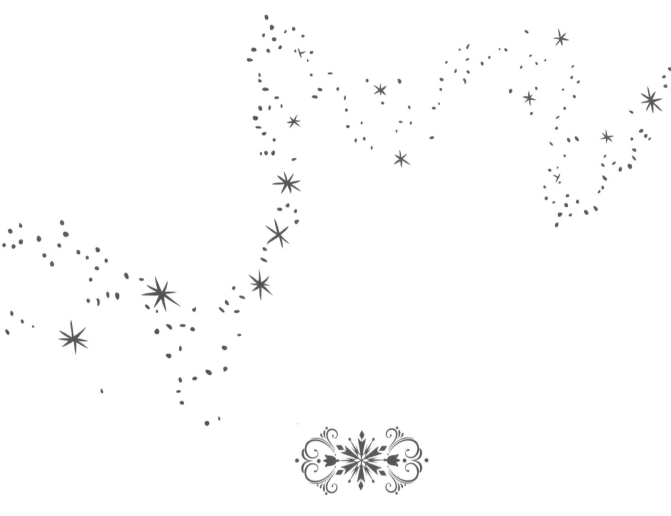

Published by Disney Press, an imprint of Disney Book Group. No part of this book may be reproduced or transmitted in any form or by any means, electronic or mechanical, including photocopying, recording, or by any information storage and retrieval system, without written permission from the publisher. For information address Disney Press, 1101 Flower Street, Glendale, California 91201.

Printed in the United States of America
First Hardcover Edition, January 2016
1 3 5 7 9 10 8 6 4 2

Library of Congress Control Number: 2015947455
FAC-038091-15324
ISBN 978-1-4847-6770-2

disneybooks.com

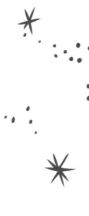

"That's no blizzard. That's my sister."
—Anna

THE KINGDOM OF ARENDELLE WAS A BUSY and happy place, nestled among the mountains and fjords of the far north. At night, the northern lights often lit up the skies in beautiful patterns.

But the king and queen lived with a secret worry.

Their eldest daughter, Elsa, had a magical power.
She could freeze things and create snow and ice with
her hands!

Anna, their younger daughter, adored her big sister. One
night, Anna convinced Elsa to sneak into the Great Hall
and create a winter wonderland!

But while the girls were playing, Elsa accidentally hit
Anna with a blast of icy magic. The little girl fell to the
ground, unconscious. A white streak appeared in her hair.
Frightened for her sister, Elsa called out for help.

The king and queen rushed the girls to the realm of the trolls, mysterious healers who knew about magic.

A wise old troll named Grand Pabbie was able to cure little Anna by changing her memories so she couldn't remember Elsa's magic. He also warned that Elsa's powers would grow stronger. "There is beauty in it but also great danger," he said. "Fear will be her enemy."

Back in Arendelle, the king and queen locked the castle gates to keep people out. No one could discover Elsa's secret.

Anna played alone while Elsa worked to control her powers.

Whenever Elsa had strong feelings,
though, the magic spilled out. The king
gave her gloves to hold it back, but Elsa
was afraid she might hurt someone by
accident. She even avoided Anna, to
keep her little sister safe.

Anna missed her sister. As the years went by, she kept asking Elsa to play. But Elsa always said she was busy.

Then, when the girls were teenagers, the king and queen were lost in a storm at sea. The sisters felt more alone—and apart—than ever.

When Elsa came of age, it was her duty to become queen. On a summer day, and for one day only, the gates of the castle were opened to celebrate the coronation.

Anna was thrilled at the chance to meet new people—and maybe even fall in love.

But Elsa was worried about being
the center of attention. What if her
powers accidentally came out?

Anna slipped outside and strolled around the
kingdom. A handsome visitor—Prince Hans of the
Southern Isles—accidentally bumped into her on his
horse. Hans and Anna were instantly smitten with each
other.

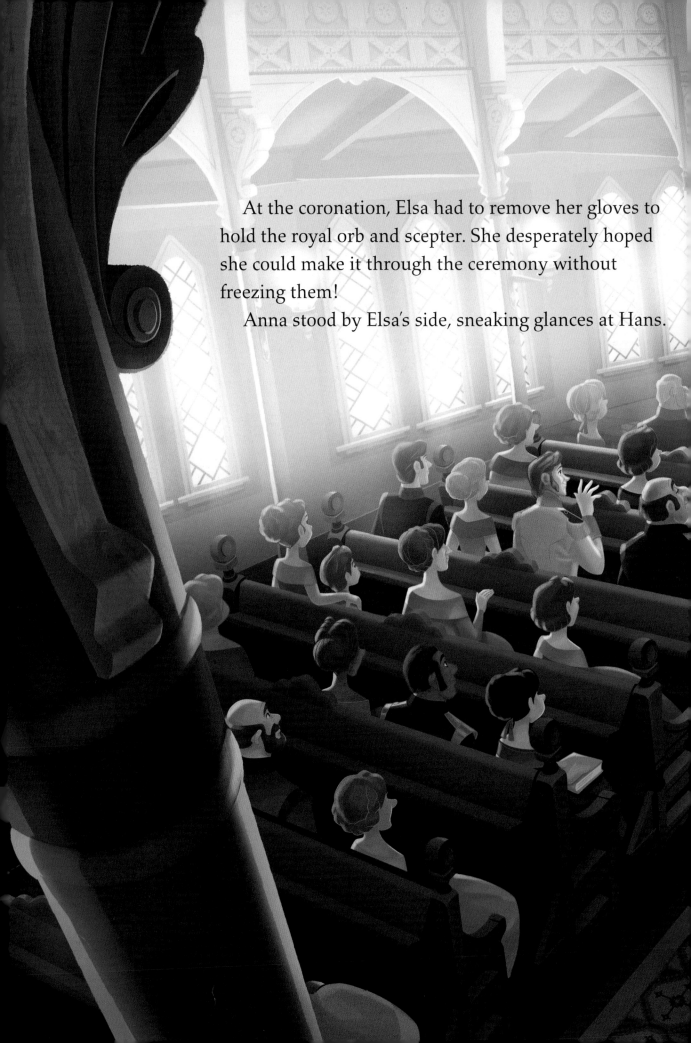

At the coronation, Elsa had to remove her gloves to hold the royal orb and scepter. She desperately hoped she could make it through the ceremony without freezing them!

Anna stood by Elsa's side, sneaking glances at Hans.

At the Coronation Ball, Hans and Anna spent every moment together.
It was love at first sight . . . so they got engaged!

Elsa was incredulous. "You can't marry a man you just met," she scoffed.

"You can if it's true love," Anna insisted.

"My answer is no," Elsa said firmly, refusing to allow the marriage.

Elsa started to leave the room,
but Anna grabbed her hand—and
accidentally pulled off her glove.

Anna kept arguing. "I can't live like this anymore!"
She asked Elsa, "Why do you shut me out?"

"Enough!" Elsa cried.

A freezing blast shot from Elsa's bare hand, sending
a sheet of ice across the ballroom! Everyone stared in
disbelief.

Elsa fled the castle, terrified that she might hurt someone. "Stay away from me," she warned the townspeople.

Everything she touched turned to ice as she ran. Even the fjord froze, trapping all the ships in place, as she stepped onto the water.

The ice continued to spread throughout the kingdom, causing an uproar
among the villagers. Meanwhile, Elsa climbed high into the mountains.
With no one else to worry about, she let all her powers loose. A blizzard
flew around her as she created ice sculptures, made a snowman, and even
transformed the way she looked.

As she neared the top of the mountain, Elsa created a magnificent, shining ice palace. She felt like the person she was always meant to be! She was alone, but she was also, at long last, entirely herself.

Anna, meanwhile, couldn't wait to reunite with her sister. Now that Elsa's secret was out, they could finally be close again! Leaving Hans in charge of Arendelle, she got on her horse and set out after Elsa.

The storm made the journey difficult, especially when Anna's horse threw her into the snow. Luckily, she spotted a small building ahead.

Inside Wandering Oaken's Trading Post and Sauna, Anna gathered up boots and some warm clothes.

Then a young man named Kristoff trudged in. He needed winter supplies.

Kristoff was an ice harvester, and he was very
unhappy that the surprise storm coming from the
North Mountain was ruining his business! Anna just
knew the storm would lead her to Elsa.

Later that evening, Anna found Kristoff in the stable
with his reindeer, Sven. She asked that he take her up
the North Mountain.

Finally, Kristoff agreed. "We leave at dawn," he said.

"We leave now," Anna insisted. "Right now."

As they started up the mountain, they heard wolves. While Anna helped Kristoff fight them off, Sven leapt over a deep gorge to escape.

The sled crashed onto the rocks below, but Anna, Kristoff, and Sven were safe.

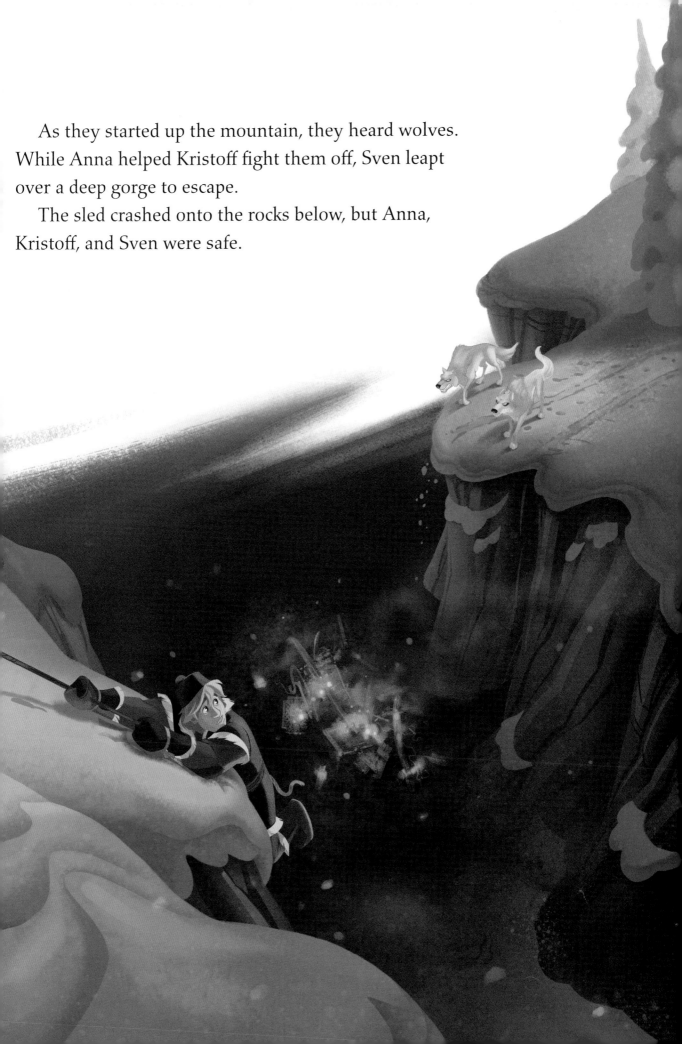

When dawn broke, Anna and Kristoff could see Arendelle far below, at the bottom of the mountain.

To their dismay, the kingdom was still locked in winter.

They hiked farther into the forest, where Elsa's icy powers had created a spectacular scene.

"I never knew winter could be so . . . beautiful," Anna said in wonder. "But it's so white," someone added. "How about a little color? I'm thinking like maybe some crimson, chartreuse. . . ."

Behind them was a living snowman! "I'm Olaf," he said, and he explained that Elsa had made him.

Anna asked Olaf to lead them to her sister. "We need Elsa to bring back summer."

"I've always loved the idea of summer," said Olaf, smiling. "The warm sun on my face . . . getting a gorgeous tan . . ."

But Anna and Kristoff both had the same thought: summer would not be good for a snowman.

Back in Arendelle, Anna's horse had returned without her. Hans organized a search party to go find her.

Meanwhile, Olaf found a stairway made of ice leading straight to Elsa's palace.

"Whoa," said Anna in awe as they reached the top. The palace was amazing!

But Elsa wasn't happy to see Anna. She was afraid of hurting her sister.

Then Anna explained that Arendelle needed Elsa's help. The kingdom was freezing, and no one knew what to do.

Now Elsa was frightened.
She admitted that she couldn't unfreeze the kingdom, because she didn't know how!

Anna was sure they could figure it out together, but Elsa just grew more upset. Frustrated, Elsa cried out, "I can't!"

An icy blast shot across the room and hit Anna in the chest!

Kristoff rushed to help Anna.
"I think we should go," he said.
"No! I'm not leaving without you,
Elsa!" insisted Anna.
"Yes, you are," Elsa replied,
conjuring up a giant snowman.

"Hey, you made me a little brother," Olaf said happily. "I'm going to name you Marshmallow!"

Elsa ordered the huge snowman to escort Anna and her companions off the mountain. But after Anna hit him with a snowball, he decided to chase them instead!

The friends ran until they reached
a cliff, and then they lowered
themselves down the side. But
Marshmallow grabbed the rope and
pulled them back up. Anna did the
only thing she could think of: she cut
the rope!

Luckily, Anna, Kristoff, and Olaf landed safely in a soft snowdrift below. But something was wrong with Anna: her hair was turning white.

"It's because she struck you with her powers, isn't it?" Kristoff asked.

Concerned about Anna, Kristoff came up with a plan. "We need to go see my friends," he said. "They can help."

Back at the ice palace, Elsa tried to figure out how she could unfreeze Arendelle. She was upset, which made the storm even worse. Hans and the rest of Anna's search party could see the growing storm over the North Mountain. They headed straight for it.

As night fell, Kristoff led Anna, Olaf, and Sven into a rocky valley, where they met his friends—the trolls.

They were practically Kristoff's family. He knew they could help Anna. The trolls were very excited to meet her. They thought she was a great match for Kristoff. Love brings out the best in everyone!

But Grand Pabbie realized that Anna was hurt.

He said that Elsa had put ice in Anna's heart, which would make her freeze solid within a day. But there was still hope. "An act of true love can thaw a frozen heart," he explained.

Olaf and Kristoff decided to take Anna back home. Surely Prince Hans could break the spell with true love's kiss.

At that same moment, Hans and the search party were arriving at Elsa's ice palace. Marshmallow tried to protect the queen, but the mob attacked him.

They went for Elsa next. With a huge blast of ice, she pinned one of the men against the wall. Just then, Hans called out, "Don't be the monster they think you are!"

Elsa realized she had let her magic go too far. She let her hands drop, and the men were safe.

But then one aimed a crossbow at Elsa! Hans pushed it aside so the arrow hit the chandelier, which fell with a crash, knocking Elsa unconscious.

Elsa woke up in a cell in the castle. Gazing out the window, she was shocked to see how her storm had damaged the kingdom.

When she asked for Anna, Hans said her sister hadn't returned.

Outside, Anna, Kristoff, and Olaf were hurrying
down the mountain. Kristoff was worried. It was clear
that Anna was getting weaker.

At the castle gates, he passed her to the royal servants. He was starting to realize that he cared deeply about Anna, but he knew that her true love, Hans, could make her well again.

The servants rushed Anna to the library, where Hans had been meeting with the dignitaries.

Shivering, Anna explained what Elsa's icy blast had done and how his kiss could cure her. "Only an act of true love can save me," she said.

"Oh, Anna," Hans sneered. "If only there was someone out there who loved you."

As he doused the fire, Hans explained that he had pretended to love Anna to take over Arendelle. All that was left, he told her, was to get rid of Elsa. "Summer will return, and the kingdom will be mine!"

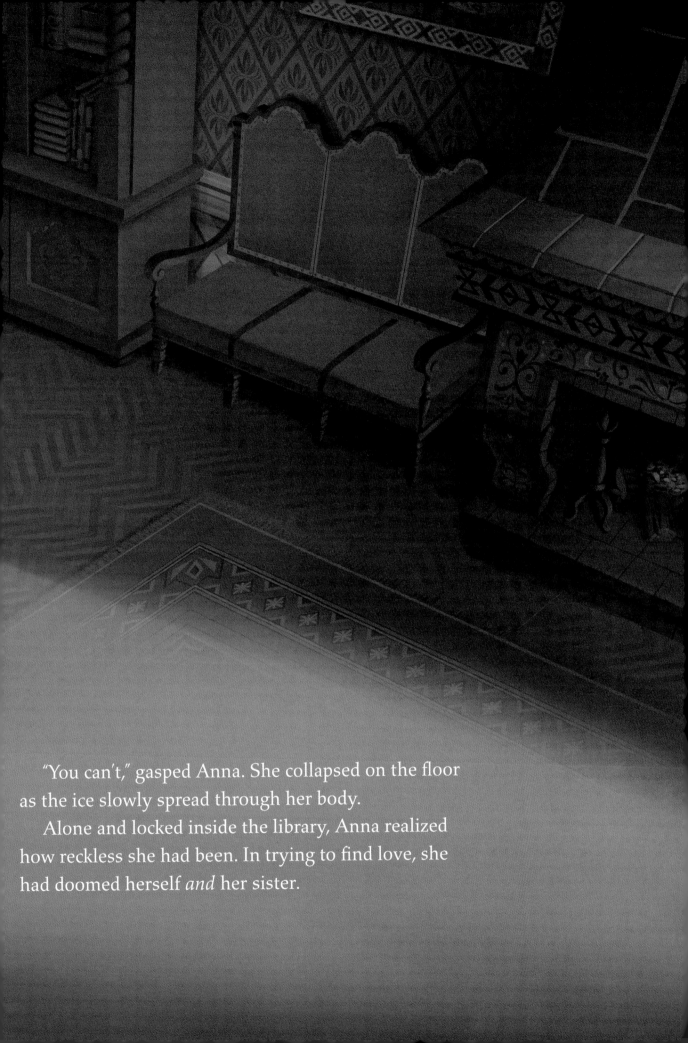

"You can't," gasped Anna. She collapsed on the floor
as the ice slowly spread through her body.

Alone and locked inside the library, Anna realized
how reckless she had been. In trying to find love, she
had doomed herself *and* her sister.

Hans returned to the dignitaries and told them that Elsa had killed Anna! He continued lying, describing how he and Anna had exchanged marriage vows before she died.

"I charge Queen Elsa with treason and sentence her to death," he declared.

In the dungeon, all Elsa could think about was getting away from Arendelle. It was the only way to protect everyone from her powers. Elsa became so upset that she froze the whole dungeon and escaped!

Meanwhile, Kristoff was heading up the mountain, but Sven forced him to stop. The reindeer thought that Kristoff was Anna's real true love.

Then Kristoff saw a violent storm over Arendelle.

He ran back toward the kingdom. He had to help Anna!

Just when Anna had given up all hope, Olaf arrived. The snowman lit a fire, even though Anna worried that he might melt. "Some people are worth melting for," he said.

Then Olaf looked out the window and saw Kristoff returning. The snowman realized that Kristoff was the true love who could save Anna!

Olaf helped Anna outside, and she spotted Kristoff across the frozen fjord. If she could reach Kristoff in time, she would be saved!

But then she saw something else: Hans was about to strike Elsa with his sword!

With her remaining strength, Anna threw herself in front of Elsa. Hans's sword came down just as Anna's body froze to solid ice. With a loud *CLANK*, the blade shattered.

Elsa wrapped her arms around her frozen sister. "Oh, Anna," she sobbed.

Then something amazing happened: Anna began to thaw! "You sacrificed yourself for me?" Elsa asked.

"I love you," replied Anna weakly.

"An act of true love will thaw a frozen heart," Olaf said, realizing what had happened.

That was when Elsa realized that love could bring back summer. She raised her arms, and the snow melted away. The people of Arendelle cheered. They had seen everything that had happened.

But Olaf was melting, too! Elsa quickly made him his own little snow cloud to keep him safe.

Hans was astonished to see Anna alive. "Anna?" he
asked. "But she froze your heart!"

"The only frozen heart around here is yours!" Anna
said, and sent him reeling with one punch.

With summer restored, the visiting ships sailed away, and Arendelle returned to normal—but now the castle gates were open for good!

Anna replaced Kristoff's sled and his supplies. But he wasn't anxious to leave—especially when Anna surprised him with a kiss.

Elsa created an ice-skating rink in the castle and welcomed the whole kingdom. Everyone had a wonderful time skating with Queen Elsa and Princess Anna.

At long last, the kingdom of Arendelle was a happy place once more.

To be continued . . .